For Cathy Berner —MB

For Jim, Ken, and Tamar —GP

VIKING
An imprint of Penguin Random House LLC, New York

First published in the United States of America by Viking,
an imprint of Penguin Random House LLC, 2020

LIBRARY OF CONGRESS CATALOGING-IN-PUBLICATION DATA IS AVAILABLE
ISBN 9780593113882

Manufactured in China
Book design by Greg Pizzoli and Jim Hoover   Set in Clarion MT Pro

10   9   8   7   6   5   4   3   2   1

GOES WEST

Mac Barnett & Greg Pizzoli

Viking

1.

DUDE RANCH

The Lady and Jack
take a train west.

They will stay for three days at a dude ranch.

This is the dude ranch.

It is next to a bank.

OK! Well, what could
go wrong with that?

2.

SLIM

This is Slim.
Howdy, Slim!

Slim is a ranch hand.
(A ranch hand works
at a ranch.)

Slim, meet the Lady!

Slim, meet Jack!

Slim takes off his hat.
He says, "Howdy, ma'am."
He smiles at the Lady.
He kisses her hand.

Jack, are you mad?

Why are you mad, Jack?

Why are you mad?

Slim says, "Let me give you a hand with your bags."

Slim picks up one bag.
He says, "Kid, grab the rest."

Why are you mad, Jack?
Why are you mad?

3.

THE BANK

A bell in the night!
A bell in the dark!
A bell at the bank!

The Lady wakes up.
She runs to the bank.

What is up?

What is wrong?

A bandit just tried to rob the town's bank!

Slim stopped the bandit.
Good job, Slim!

You the man!
Tell us what a good
job you did!

"I heard the bell and
I rushed to the bank.

I saw the bandit
bust into the safe.

I cried out and he dropped these three sacks of gold.

I tried to rope him,
but he was too fast."

"I got a look at him, though.
He looked just like this!"

Say! Where have we
seen a face like that?

4.

ROPE TRICKS

The Lady and Slim
ride horses all day.

Jack has to stay back,
back near the ranch.

It is hot. It is dry.
There are rocks.
There is sand.

There are cows
and a cactus.

There is more sand.

Do not be sad, Jack.
Do not get mad.

Hey! Show us
some rope tricks!

Since we're in the West,
rope that there cactus.
It looks like a man!

Oops! You missed, Jack!

Jack, try again!

Oh. Well. You missed.

Jack, you missed. Again.

Try one more time, Jack.

Throw it as far as you can!

Wow! That was far, Jack.

Where did your rope land?

Oh. You roped
a bull, Jack.

This could be bad.

5.

THE
MESS

Slim and the Lady
eat beans in the mess.
(The mess is the room
where you eat on the
ranch.)

Slim takes out a ring.
He gets down on one knee.

"I love you," Slim says.
He asks for her hand.

"Spend your life with me, Lady!"

Wow! Slim moves fast.

Will the Lady say no?

Will the Lady say yes?

The Lady says, "Maybe."

"Sleep on it," Slim says.

"Tell me tomorrow.
Keep the ring until then."

The Lady smiles at Slim
and gives him a kiss.

Why are you mad, Jack?
Why are you mad?

6.

THE
BANDIT

The Lady lies
awake in her bed.

She looks at her ring.

The bell rings out!

Quick!
To the bank!
Fast!

Look! There is the bandit!
Tied up by the safe!

Lift up his hat!

Let's see who it is!

It is Slim! Oh wow!
The bandit is Slim!

It was a frame job.
Slim tried to blame Jack!

Why did you do it, Slim?
Why would you frame Jack?

"I love the Lady.
I do not love Jack.
So I thought I would frame him.

Jack would get sent to the can."
(The can is what they call jail
in the West.)

"Then this gold would be mine.
Me and the Lady could buy our
own ranch.

Just us two.
And not Jack."

Wow! Slim is a bad man!

But who stopped
the bandit?

Who roped this bad man?

Jack!

Jack roped Slim!

The Law Lady pins a
gold star to Jack's chest.

The man from the bank
pats Jack on the back.

The Law Lady says,
"I will put Slim in the can."

The Bank Man says,
"I will put the three
sacks in the safe."

Wait. Three sacks?
There are just two
sacks here.

Where is the third sack?

It was right on Slim's lap.

"Jack took the loot
right off of my lap!"

Jack! Where is Jack?

Jack is long gone.

He is on a train east.

He and the Lady
ride in first class.

HOW TO DRAW...
SLIM!

IF YOU WANT MORE JACK, READ:

A JACK BOOK

HI, JACK!

Mac Barnett & Greg Pizzoli

A JACK BOOK

JACK BLASTS OFF!

Mac Barnett & Greg Pizzoli

A JACK BOOK

JACK AT BAT

Mac Barnett & Greg Pizzoli